MW01079085

First published in Belgium and Holland by Clavis Uitgeverij, Hasselt – Amsterdam, 2013
Copyright © 2013, Clavis Uitgeverij

English translation from the Dutch by Clavis Publishing Inc. New York
Copyright © 2014 for the English language edition: Clavis Publishing Inc. New York

Visit us on the web at www.clavisbooks.com

No part of this publication may be reproduced or stored in a retrieval system, or transmitted
in any form or by any means, electronic, mechanical, photocopying, recording, or otherwise,
without the prior written permission of the publisher, except in the case of brief quotations
embodied in critical articles and reviews.
For information regarding permissions, write to Clavis Publishing, info-US@clavisbooks.com

Ian Is Moving written and illustrated by Pauline Oud
Original title: *Kas gaat verhuizen*
Translated from the Dutch by Clavis Publishing

ISBN 978-1-60537-174-0

This book was printed in February 2014 at Proost, Everdongenlaan 23, 2300 Turnhout, Belgium

First Edition
10 9 8 7 6 5 4 3 2 1

Clavis Publishing supports the First Amendment and celebrates the right to read

Ian

is Moving

Pauline Oud

Clavis

NEW YORK

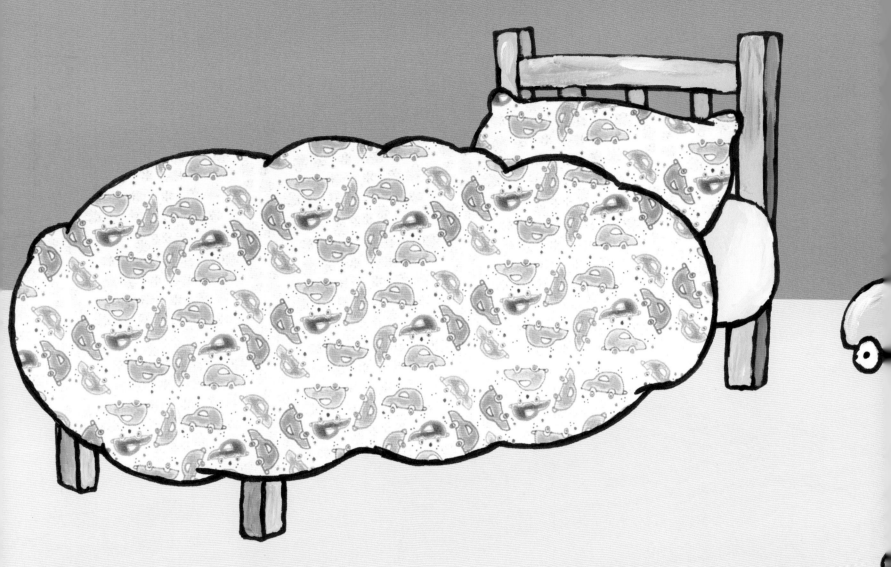

Today is a special day.
Ian is moving to another house with his mom
and dad. There's a lot of work to be done.
Mom and Dad are very busy. Ian is helping
them. He puts all his favorite things in a big
box. "Look here, Flap," Ian says to his cuddly
rabbit, "this beautiful book, my ball, my train
and my car are coming with us to the new house!"

Here's the moving van!
Strong moving men carry all the boxes,
cupboards and lamps into the van.

"Look!" Ian yells. "That's my bed!"

"Of course," Mom says, "we wouldn't forget your bed."

Ian can carry his own box to the moving van.

"Wow," one of the strong men says.

"Can you really carry that heavy box by yourself?"

"Yes," Ian says quietly.

"Then one day you'll be as strong as I am!" the man smiles.

Mom puts the last few things in a box.
The house is almost empty.
Only the couch is left in the living room.
"Why aren't we taking the couch with us?" Ian asks.
"It's old," Mom answers.
"There's a new couch in the new house,
you'll like it as much as this one."
Ian strokes the cushions one more time.
"Goodbye couch. Goodbye room," he says.
"I'm going to the new house now."

Dad drives the
car to the new
house. Ian and
Mom travel in the
large moving van.
"Goodbye house!" Ian yells from
the window. "Goodbye neighbor!
Goodbye Spotty!" Mom and Ian wave.
Spotty wags his tail. "Goodbye swing! Goodbye street!
We're moving to a new house!"

When they get to the new house,
Ian grabs his box from the van.
The strong men carry all the furniture
and boxes inside.

"There's my bed!" Ian shouts.
"Where do you want us to put it?"
a moving man asks.
"In the bathroom? Next to the toilet?"
"No," Ian laughs. "In my new bedroom!"

"Will you help me?" Dad asks.
Carefully Ian unpacks his box.
"Look here, Flap," says Ian, "this is our new bedroom.
This book and this car will also live here."
Dad puts everything where it belongs.
Everything has its own place in the new room.
Soon the room starts to look comfortable.

When everything is in the house, the moving men leave.
Ian sits on the new couch in the living room.
"The new couch is very soft," Ian says. He strokes the cushions.
"Sure," Mom nods, "the new couch is just as nice as the old one."

Bam, bam, bam. What's making that noise?
"Quickly, go and have a look!" Mom says.

"Hi Granddad!" Ian says as he runs into the new garden.

"Well, you're just in time!" Granddad says.

"You can help me hammer in the last few nails."

"A new swing!" Ian yells happily.

"Yep," Granddad nods, "and I fit right into it.
You can push me!"

"No," Ian laughs. "That swing is not for you, it's for me!"

When Granddad and Ian are done hammering,
Ian climbs into the swing.
"Hi there!" they hear.
Who's that behind the garden fence?
It's Sarah, from Ian's school.
"This is my new house and this is my swing!"
Ian tells her joyfully, "I live here!"
"And I live there!" Sarah says as she points to the house
on the other side of the street.
"Do you want to try the swing?" Ian asks.

"Dinner's ready!"
Dad calls a bit later.
Even with all the moving,
there's food on the table.
Fries!
Ian takes a big bite.
"Will there be enough fries
and salad?" Granddad asks.

"Because we're as hungry as moving men, aren't we?" He winks at Ian.
"Yeah!" Ian laughs.
Wow, the fries taste great in the new house.

After dinner, Ian goes to bath.
The new tub is very large and
filled with bubbles.
But where is Ian's rubber duck?
"Did we leave Duck in the old
house?" he asks anxiously.
"And my bathrobe? Have we
forgotten my bathrobe
as well?"

Then Ian hears Granddad.
"Hey, this bathrobe doesn't fit me.
It must be Ian's.
Quack, quack! Look here, Duck,
this is your new tub!"

Ian climbs into his own cozy bed.
Mom reads him a story from his favorite book.
Flap and the large giraffe listen as well.
"The new house is great," Ian says.
"Tomorrow, Sarah is coming
to play in the swing again!"
"It's nice that Sarah is your new neighbor," Mom says,
and she gives Ian a kiss.
"Goodnight, Ian,
sleep well in
your new house!"

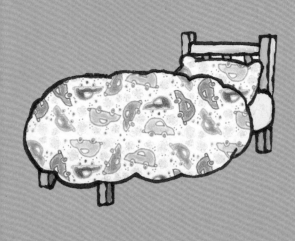

Which toys belong to Ian?

What is Ian taking in his box?

What is staying behind in the old house?

Which bed belongs to Ian?

What does Grandpa make for Ian?

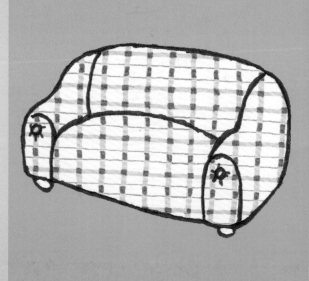